The Grandpa Book

TODD PARR

Megan Tingley Books
LITTLE, BROWN AND COMPANY
New York   Boston

Todd Parr is the author of more than thirty books
for children, including the *New York Times* bestselling
The I Love You Book. He lives in Berkeley, California.

Also by Todd Parr:

The I Love You Book

It's Okay to Be Different

The Earth Book

The Peace Book

We Belong Together

The Mommy Book

The Daddy Book

The Grandma Book

The Family Book

Reading Makes You Feel Good

The Feelings Book

The Feel Good Book

For a complete list of
Todd's books and more information, please visit
www.toddparr.com and www.planetcolorbytoddparr.com.

Copyright © 2006 by Todd Parr

Little, Brown and Company • Hachette Book Group • 237 Park Avenue, New York, NY 10017 • Visit our website at www.lb-kids.com

Little, Brown and Company is a division of Hachette Book Group, Inc. • The Little, Brown name and logo are trademarks of Hachette Book Group, Inc.

First Paperback Edition: May 2011
First published in hardcover in April 2006 by Little, Brown and Company

Library of Congress Cataloging-in-Publication Data
Parr, Todd.
The grandpa book / by Todd Parr. — 1st ed.
p. cm.
"Megan Tingley Books"
Summary: Presents the different ways grandfathers show their
grandchildren love, from putting extra marshmallows in hot chocolate
to sending cards and telling stories.
ISBN 978-0-316-05801-8 (hc) / ISBN 978-0-316-07043-0 (pb)

[1. Grandfathers—Fiction. 2. Grandparent and child—Fiction.] I. Title.
PZ7.P2447Gra 2006

[E]—dc22   2004027847

10 9 8 7 6 5 4 3 2

QUAL

Printed in China

This book is dedicated to my Grandpa Parr, who wasn't around long enough. Thanks for helping me draw.

And to my Grandpa Logan, who taught me how to fish and plant a garden. Thanks for forgiving me for all those soda cans I used to stuff under the cushion of your favorite chair.

 Love,
Todd

Some grandpas collect a lot of different things

Some grandpas have a lot
of pictures of you

Some grandpas put extra money in your piggy bank

Some grandpas put extra marshmallows in your hot chocolate

All grandpas like to

tell you stories

Some grandpas talk really loudly

Some grandpas send you cards.

Some grandpas can wiggle their ears

Some grandpas let you try on their glasses

All grandpas like to

make you laugh

Some grandpas take you to school

Some grandpas take you to the park

Some grandpas live with a grandma

Some grandpas live with their friends

Some grandpas like to walk

Some grandpas like to drive

All grandpas like to

hold and hug you

Grandpas are very special. They make you laugh and teach you new things. Be sure to tell them how much you Love them.

♥ Love, Todd